For Elena and Natalie —A.W.

For Kastor & Pollux,
my little adventurers —C.M.

THIS IS A BORZOI BOOK PUBLISHED BY ALFRED A. KNOPF.
Text copyright © 2025 by Allison Wortche
Jacket art and interior illustrations copyright © 2025 by Cat Min

All rights reserved. Published in the United States by Alfred A. Knopf, an imprint of Random House Children's Books, a division of Penguin Random House LLC, 1745 Broadway, New York, NY 10019.
Knopf, Borzoi Books, and the colophon are registered trademarks of Penguin Random House LLC.

Visit us on the Web! rhcbooks.com
Educators and librarians, for a variety of teaching tools, visit us at RHTeachersLibrarians.com

Library of Congress Cataloging-in-Publication Data is available upon request.
ISBN 978-0-593-70482-0 (trade) — ISBN 978-0-593-70483-7 (lib. bdg.) — ISBN 978-0-593-70484-4 (ebook)

The text of this book is set in 16-point Brandon.
The illustrations were created using watercolors and colored pencils on paper and Procreate.

Editor: Nancy Siscoe Designer: Sarah Hokanson Copy Editor: Artie Bennett
Managing Editor: Jake Eldred Production Manager: Jennifer Moreno

MANUFACTURED IN CHINA 10 9 8 7 6 5 4 3 2 1 First Edition

The authorized representative in the EU for product safety and compliance is Penguin Random House Ireland, Morrison Chambers, 32 Nassau Street, Dublin D02 YH68, Ireland, https://eu-contact.penguin.ie.

Random House Children's Books supports the First Amendment and celebrates the right to read.

Penguin Random House LLC values and supports copyright. Copyright fuels creativity, encourages diverse voices, promotes free speech, and creates a vibrant culture. Thank you for buying an authorized edition of this book and for complying with copyright laws by not reproducing, scanning, or distributing any part in any form without permission. You are supporting writers and allowing Penguin Random House to publish books for every reader. Please note that no part of this book may be used or reproduced in any manner for the purpose of training artificial intelligence technologies or systems.

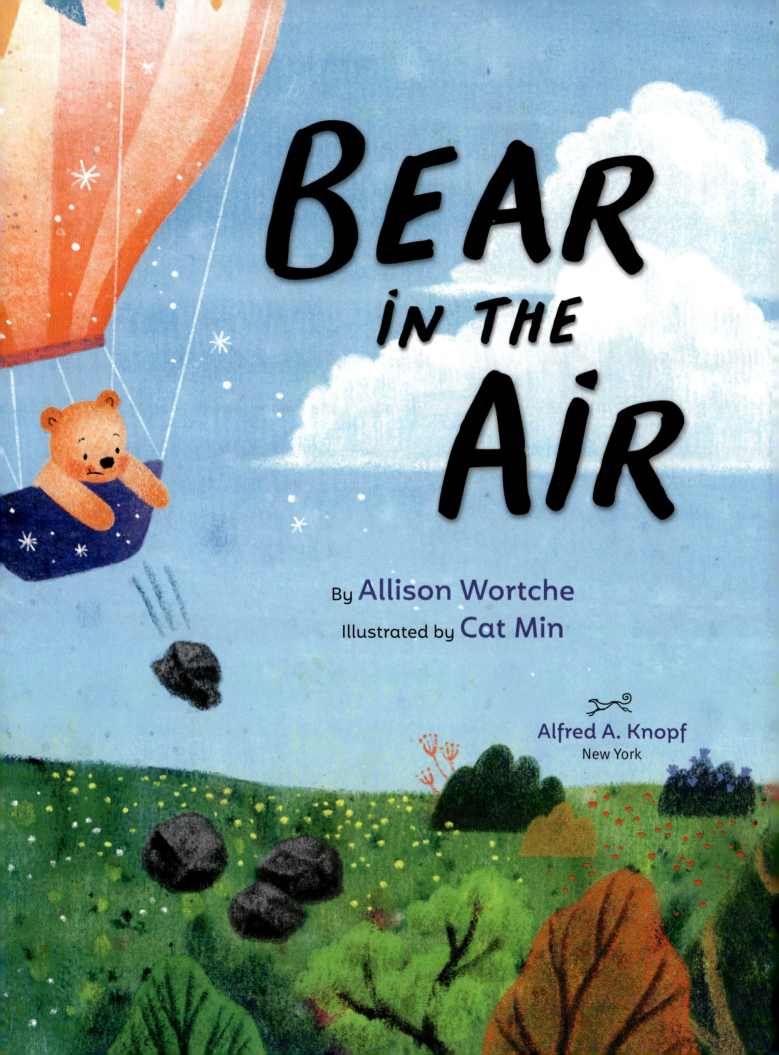

This is Bear.

He's in the air!

He likes it up there.

Bear floats among the clouds,
far above
fields and forests,
sunflowers and streams,
everything that looks so small.

He spots his friends below.

"Helloooo! I'm in the air!"

"So high!" says Fox.
"So brave!" says Hare.
Bear waves.

"Hey, Bear!" his sisters call.

They've found the tallest, finest climbing tree around. But Bear is
even
higher.
"Want to climb with us?"

"Ahoy there, Bear!" Goat shouts from his mountain. "Would you like to come down for some cookies?"

"No, thank you!" says Bear.
"I'm on an adventure!"

Bear's tummy does feel a little grumbly. He forgot to pack granola bars.

"Care for a swim, Bear?"

"No, thank you. It's nice and breezy up here!"

Actually, it *is* getting a bit hot. . . .

"Hey, Bear! Come join me— I have an extra chair!"

"No, thank you! I like standing!"
The chair looks comfy.
Bear scrunches up his toes.

The balloon drifts over the village square.

"Still up there, Bear?"
"Yup."
"Well, it's time for the fair!"

Cotton candy puffs.
Ooey-gooey s'mores.
Dancing with friends!
Bear loves the fair.

But he has a secret
that he doesn't want to share.

"Where are you going, Bear?!"

Bear is all alone in the air.

"I might need a little help,"
he whispers into the wind.

Then he takes a big, brave breath.
His voice echoes over fields and forests,
sunflowers and streams:

"I don't know how to get DOWN! DOWN down down..."

The sun begins to sink,
and the sky
fills
with cotton candy.

Bear floats
toward Goat's empty mountain.
It'll be me and the moon soon, he thinks
when just below . . .

"We've got you,

Bear sits in a circle of friends.
"Maybe I'll go sailing next," he says, mouth full of ooey-gooey marshmallow.
"Imagine me on the sea."

Bear was in the air.
And he liked it up there!
But tonight?
This is
right
where
he wants to be.